Hiya! My name Thudd. Best robot friend of Drewd. Thudd know lots of stuff. Why garbage get stinky. How bug walk on ceiling. Where bird get feathers. How things fly.

Drewd like to invent stuff. Thudd help! But Drewd make lots of mistakes. Today Drewd try out garbage-shrinking machine. Thudd worried. Want to see what happen? Turn page, please!

ANDREW LOST

BY J. C. GREENBURG

ILLUSTRATED
BY JAN GERARDI

IN THE GARBAGE

13

A STEPPING STONE BOOK™

Random House 🏠 New York

To Dan, Zack, and the real Andrew,
with a galaxy of love.
To the children who read these books: I wish
you wonderful questions. Questions are
telescopes into the universe!
—J.C.G.

To Cathy Goldsmith, with many thanks.
—J.G.

Text copyright © 2006 by J. C. Greenburg.
Illustrations copyright © 2006 by Jan Gerardi.
All rights reserved. Published in the United States by Random House Children's Books, a division of Random House, Inc., New York.

RANDOM HOUSE and colophon are registered trademarks and A STEPPING STONE BOOK and colophon are trademarks of Random House, Inc. ANDREW LOST is a trademark of J. C. Greenburg.

www.randomhouse.com/kids/AndrewLost
www.AndrewLost.com

Educators and librarians, for a variety of teaching tools, visit us at www.randomhouse.com/teachers

Library of Congress Cataloging-in-Publication Data
Greenburg, J. C. (Judith C.)
In the garbage / by J. C. Greenburg ; illustrated by
Jan Gerardi. — 1st ed.
    p. cm. — (Andrew Lost ; 13) "A Stepping Stone book."
SUMMARY: Andrew, his cousin Judy, and Thudd the robot wind up at a garbage dump when Andrew's latest invention, the Goa Constrictor, shrinks them to the size of beetles and swallows them.
ISBN 0-375-83562-8 (trade) — ISBN 0-375-93562-2 (lib. bdg.)
[1. Refuse and refuse disposal—Fiction. 2. Inventions—Fiction.
3. Size—Fiction. 4. Cousins—Fiction.]
I. Gerardi, Jan, ill. II. Title. III. Series: Greenburg, J. C. (Judith C.).
Andrew Lost ; v 13.
PZ7.G82785Inw 2006   [Fic]—dc22   2005021776

Printed in the United States of America
First Edition 10 9 8 7 6

THUDD

CONTENTS

ANDREW'S WORLD

Andrew Dubble

Andrew is ten years old, but he's been inventing things since he was four. Andrew's inventions usually get him in trouble, like the time he invented the Aroma-Rama. It was supposed to make homes and offices smell like flowers. Instead, it made everything smell like stinky feet!

Andrew's newest invention is supposed to save the world from getting buried in garbage. But a nasty classmate could get *Andrew* buried in garbage!

Judy Dubble

Judy is Andrew's thirteen-year-old cousin.

She's been snuffled into a dog's nose, pooped out of a whale, and had her pajamas chewed by a Tyrannosaurus—all because of Andrew!

Thudd

The Handy Ultra-Digital Detective. Thudd is a super-smart robot and Andrew's best friend. He has helped save Andrew and Judy from the exploding sun, a giant squid, and a monster asteroid. But can he keep them from getting thrown out with the garbage?

Uncle Al

Andrew and Judy's uncle is a top-secret scientist. He invented Thudd. Uncle Al and Andrew have worked on many inventions together. Too bad Uncle Al wasn't around to help Andrew with this one. Where *is* Uncle Al, anyway?

Jeremy Bogart

Jeremy goes to school with Andrew and Judy. It won't take you long to figure out why kids call him "Germy Booger"!

The Goa Constrictor

This giant fake snake is Andrew's newest invention. Goa is short for **Garbage Goes Away**. The Goa is supposed to keep the world from getting buried in garbage by squashing rotten vegetables, green meat, and dirty paper dishes down to microscopic size. Unfortunately for Andrew, the Goa doesn't just shrink garbage. In two minutes and one stinky burp, the Goa can shrink anything—and anyone.

SSSSSSSSSSSS . . .

"Yerrrrghhh!" groaned ten-year-old Andrew Dubble. He was dragging a heavy black bag through his classroom door. The bag was squirming!

No one else was in the room.

"Wowzers!" said Andrew. "We've finally got the place to ourselves."

Ch . . . ch . . . ch . . . ch . . . ch . . .

Angry screams were coming from a cage behind Andrew. It was Harry and Howard, the class guinea pigs.

Andrew felt a poke inside his shirt pocket.

meep . . . "Animals afraid, Drewd," came a squeaky voice.

It was Andrew's little silver robot and best friend, Thudd. Thudd was short for The Handy Ultra-Digital Detective.

Andrew looked around the room. A forest of trees reached for the ceiling. Plants with giant leaves pressed against the windows. Plastic hamster trails zigzagged through it all.

A shelf at the back held roomy cages for mice and guinea pigs. A hairy tarantula spider the size of Andrew's hand lived in a sandy aquarium tank.

"Don't worry, Thudd," said Andrew. "I'll make sure the Goa Constrictor eats just the garbage."

Andrew checked the clock on the wall. "The cafeteria ladies said they would bring the garbage at three o'clock," he said. "We've got fifteen minutes to get ready."

Andrew untied the squirming black bag and pulled a small remote control from his pants pocket. He pressed the Slither Out button.

Sssssssssss . . . came a loud hiss from the bag. A giant brown snake head poked out. It had blinking red lights for eyes. A thin black tongue flicked from its mouth.

The huge snake slipped out of the bag. Its body was brown and yellow. It was as thick as a wastebasket and as long as a ladder.

Andrew beamed. "Wowzers schnauzers! Isn't the Goa *beautiful*?"

"Yoop! Yoop! Yoop!" said Thudd. "But gotta be careful, Drewd. Remember Atom Sucker."

Not long ago, Andrew had invented the Atom Sucker. It shrunk things by sucking the empty space out of atoms. Andrew accidentally shrunk himself so small that he got snuffled into the nose of a dog, flushed down a toilet, and almost eaten by a nasty neighbor.

Andrew laughed. "I'll never forget *that*," he said.

"Andrew!" came a voice from the hall. It was Judy, Andrew's thirteen-year-old cousin.

"And Judy will never let me forget it, either," said Andrew.

The Atom Sucker had shrunk Judy, too.

"Cheese Louise!" Judy yelled as she backed away from the doorway. "What is *that*?"

"It's my entry for the Young Inventors Contest," said Andrew. "It's called the Goa Constrictor. Goa stands for **G**arbage **Go**es **A**way."

"Then you should call it the Gga Constrictor," said Judy. "That's the *right* way to make a name from initials, Bug-Brain."

"It's my invention," said Andrew, "so I get to invent its name, too. Wait till you see the Goa in action. It swallows a giant pile of garbage, then it squeezes the empty space out of the atoms and makes the garbage super-small. I'll show you."

Suddenly the Goa Constrictor raised its head. Its tongue flicked faster.

meep . . . "Goa Constrictor smell stuff with tongue," said Thudd. "Goa Constrictor got little pits on side of face that feel heat. When garbage get rotty, garbage get warm. Goa find it."

Sssssssssssss . . .

The Goa Constrictor, red eyes blinking faster, slithered toward Judy.

"Aack!" yelled Judy, backing away. "Does it think I'm garbage or something?"

Andrew shrugged. "I don't know," he said as the Goa Constrictor zigzagged toward the door. "But it sure does smell something funny."

GERMY BOOGER

"Whoop-de-do!" hooted a tall boy in the doorway. "It's Dandy Andy's garbage gobbler!"

The Goa Constrictor quickly twisted itself around the boy's legs.

"Hey, Germy," Andrew said to the boy. He clicked the Off button on the remote. The Goa Constrictor lay still.

The tall boy shook his black hair away from his eyes. "You're beginning to talk like that tin can in your pocket, Andy."

Judy crossed her arms over her chest and frowned. "Stuff a sock in it, Jeremy Bogart," she said. "If you didn't annoy everyone all the

time, kids wouldn't call you Germy Booger."

"That's *so* unkind," said Jeremy. "I'm a really nice kid. I've even done something nice for little Andy."

Jeremy stepped into the hall and came back dragging two bulging garbage bags. The sweet-sour smell of garbage filled the room.

"See how nice I am?" said Jeremy. "I helped the cafeteria ladies by delivering these bags."

"Be prepared to be amazed, Germy," said

Andrew, pressing a button on the remote.

The Goa Constrictor raised its head and opened its jaws wide enough to swallow a toaster. The jaws opened wider and wider—wide enough to swallow an oven!

meep . . . "Snakes got special jaws," said Thudd. "Bottom jaw come apart from top jaw. Can open mouth wide, wide, wide!"

Andrew dragged one of the garbage bags close to the Goa Constrictor's mouth. "The Goa will make this garbage super-small."

"Oooooh!" said Jeremy. "A really creepy garbage gobbler. *Everybody* will want one."

"Listen, Germy," said Andrew, looking Jeremy in the eye. "Every person—including you—makes five pounds of garbage every day. That's thirty-five pounds every week. That's more than eighteen hundred pounds every year for every person!

"We need to make less garbage before we get buried in it. But until we figure out how to do that, the Goa can make garbage smaller!"

Andrew lifted the garbage bag. He poured a mess of half-eaten hot dogs, brown banana chunks, rotten grapes, chewed French fries, and ketchup-covered paper napkins into the Goa's mouth.

The Goa's bottom jaw moved in and out, dragging the garbage in fast.

When it sucked down the last potato peel, the Goa slowly closed its jaws.

Sssssssssss . . .

A giant beach-ball-sized bulge appeared behind the Goa's head and moved slowly through its body.

SSSSSSSSSSSS . . .

The hiss sounded like a bucket of water hitting a bonfire. Suddenly the Goa's mouth snapped open. Out swirled a rainbow-colored tornado that smelled like a thousand rotten eggs.

NO EXCUSES

"Ack! Ack!" coughed Judy.

"Yerf!" hollered Jeremy, pinching his nose with his fingers.

Andrew held his breath.

The tornado swirled toward the ceiling and vanished. The smell disappeared. And the bulge in the middle of the Goa Constrictor was gone.

Now the Goa's tail was twitching so fast that it seemed to disappear. As soon as the tail was still, Andrew lifted it.

"Super-duper pooper-scooper!" he shouted. "Look!"

Beneath the tail was a tiny pile of colored specks.

Andrew put down the remote and reached into his pants pocket. He pulled out a small black tube and put it up to his eye.

"Woofers!" he said. "The Goa really *did* shrink the garbage! Apple cores and paper cups are smaller than grains of sand! Some stuff is so small I can't even see it with my Tele-Mag."

"Give me that thing," said Jeremy, kneeling down on the floor. He grabbed the Tele-Mag out of Andrew's hand, put it up to his eye, and looked at the tiny pile. "It's just a big blur!" he said.

"That's because you're holding the Tele-Mag the wrong way," said Andrew. "One end is a telescope and the other end is a microscope."

Jeremy turned the tube around and examined the specks. "Okay. It's teensy-weensy garbage," he said. "Who cares?"

Andrew grabbed back the Tele-Mag and picked up the remote. "So where's *your* invention, Germy?" he asked.

"Right here," said Jeremy, getting to his feet.

He reached into his pants pocket and pulled out what looked like a black Ping-Pong ball.

"Humph," said Judy, frowning. "Just what the world is waiting for—a smooth golf ball. One that's really hard to find."

Jeremy shook his head. "You wouldn't recognize a genius idea if it landed on your brain," he said. "This is the *Excuse-O-Matic*. The world *is* waiting for this."

Jeremy clicked a silver button at the top of the black ball. "I didn't do my homework," he said slowly.

hmmmmmmmmmmm . . .

The ball hummed softly. It began to spin in Jeremy's palm.

hmmmmm . . . "My little brother ate my homework," whined a small voice from the whirling ball.

hmmmmm . . . "I got food poisoning and threw up all night."

hmmmmm . . . "A robber broke into our house and took everything, even my homework."

Jeremy clicked the silver button again and the Excuse-O-Matic was quiet.

"See?" said Jeremy. "It works for every situation—being late, losing stuff—*anything!* Everybody needs good excuses."

"*Lies,* you mean," said Judy.

Jeremy smiled. "Just other ways of looking at things," he said. "Even Dandy Andy will love this. Catch!"

He tossed the Excuse-O-Matic to Andrew.

The Excuse-O-Matic knocked the remote control out of Andrew's hand. It fell to the floor.

The red eyes of the Goa Constrictor blinked fast. It opened its jaws, scooped up the Excuse-O-Matic and the remote, and snapped its jaws shut.

"Get my Excuse-O-Matic back!" yelled Jeremy. "Or else I'll say you stole it! You'll get arrested!"

"No way!" said Judy.

Judy threw herself on the Goa Constrictor, grabbed its top jaw, and pulled.

Andrew flopped down in front of the Goa, got a grip on its bottom jaw, and looked inside.

"See anything?" asked Judy.

"Not yet," said Andrew. He snapped his mini-flashlight off his belt loop and clicked it on. "Can you pull the mouth open a little wider?"

"Uuugh!" groaned Judy, pulling harder. "I can't hold this jaw open much longer."

Andrew pushed his head and then his

shoulders into the Goa's mouth.

"Ooof!" exclaimed Judy as the top jaw snapped out of her grip. It clomped down on Andrew.

Sssssssssss . . .

The bottom jaw was moving in and out. It was pulling Andrew inside like a conveyor belt!

"Uh-oh," said Andrew. He was inside the Goa up to his chest!

Andrew could hear Jeremy laughing.

"Germy Booger, this is all your fault," said Judy. "Get over here and grab one of Andrew's legs."

"Boo*hoo*!" hooted Jeremy, walking out the door. "Dandy Andy is *your* problem. I'm going to tell Principal Smuggins. You guys are in big trouble."

Andrew felt Judy's hands gripping his ankles and yanking.

"AAAAAAAACK!" screamed Judy.

SSSSSSSSSSSS . . .

The horrible hiss was the last sound Andrew heard before his head felt like it was filled with helium and everything went black.

WHAT'S STINKIER THAN A WHALE'S INTESTINES?

Andrew was trapped in a dream.

He was in a courtroom. A jury had found him guilty of inventing the Aroma-Rama. The Aroma-Rama was supposed to make homes and stores and offices smell like a garden. Instead, it made every place smell like stinky feet.

Andrew's punishment was to clean out refrigerators for the rest of his life.

A guard brought him to a room filled with junky old refrigerators.

Andrew was cleaning the first one. He had just twisted the lid off a jar of black goo that smelled like sour milk, gasoline, and dog poop when . . .

Klunketa . . . klunketa . . . klunketa . . .

A loud clunking sound woke him up.

Andrew felt damp all over. He rubbed his eyes. The light was bright. He was leaning against a tall wall with brown and yellow tiles. And he was sitting on a pile of garbage!

The room looked familiar, but something was wrong. The ceiling looked awfully far away.

"Uh-oh," said Andrew. "The Goa shrunk us, pooped us out, and now we're sitting on the tiny garbage I shrunk before! I must be about as big as a cockroach."

meep . . . "Small cockroach," said Thudd.

Ga-nufff . . . ga-nufff . . . gnewww . . .

Andrew turned toward the sound. It was coming from a pile of dark, frizzy hair nearby. The pile was snoring!

"Judy!" said Andrew to the pile of hair.

Judy was asleep and buried up to her neck in garbage.

Klunketa . . . klunketa . . . klunketa . . .

The clunking sound was closer. Andrew pushed runny cheese and soggy crackers away from Judy's shoulders and tried to shake her awake.

Ga-nufff . . . ga-nufff . . . gnewww . . .

She shook her head but stayed sound asleep.

Klunketa . . . klunketa . . . klunketa . . .

"Whoa!" came a deep voice from the doorway. "Hey, Frank! Get a look at the fake snake! Must be for Show-and-Tell Day."

"No way, Jeff," said Frank. "It's for Take Your Fake Snake to Work Day."

The men laughed.

"Hey," said Frank. "Where's that garbage we're supposed to pick up?"

"Must be that bag next to the fake snake," said Jeff. "I'll get it."

Andrew watched the dark, heavy shoes get closer.

"I'm not even as high as the sole of his shoe," said Andrew. "He could stomp me like a bug."

"Well, look here," said Jeff. "The fake snake made fake poop! Hand me a broom and a dustpan, Frank. Thanks. I'll toss this stuff into the garbage bag."

Andrew looked up at Jeff's face. It was like looking at the carvings of the presidents on Mount Rushmore.

"HELP!" Andrew shouted. *"GET US OUT OF THE GARBAGE!"*

The dark, dirty dustpan clunked against the floor.

A wall of yellow bristles swept toward Andrew like a tsunami. Andrew covered his face with his hands and crouched in the garbage. A wave of stinky wetness crashed over him as the pile of tiny garbage was shoved into the dustpan.

Andrew felt the dustpan going up, then it tilted. Andrew was sliding fast. Suddenly he felt his stomach fluttering into his mouth. They were falling into the garbage bag!

Splat!

"Oofers!" hollered Andrew as he belly-flopped onto a regular-sized pickle at the top of the bag.

"Andrew?" Judy called sleepily from a soggy taco shell. She rubbed her eyes and yawned. "Where *are* we? It's stinkier than a whale's intestines."

"Um, we're in a garbage bag," said Andrew. "The Goa Constrictor shrunk us."

Judy rolled off her taco shell. "We're shrunk *again*!" She crawled toward Andrew. "Wait till I get my hands on you!"

Judy wiped a drop of hot sauce off her nose and shoved her face toward Andrew's. "I should have kept my New Year's resolution," she said angrily.

"What was that?" said Andrew.

"To stay at least five miles away from you at all times," said Judy.

"Listen," said Andrew. "As soon as I find the remote, we'll get out of the bag, get into the Goa Constrictor's mouth, and I'll press the Reverse button. We'll be right back to our normal size in no time."

Judy rolled her eyes. "Yeah, right," she said.

The garbage tumbled. Someone was lifting the bag. A French fry crashed down on Andrew's head. Judy got smacked in the face by a bow-tie noodle.

"Toss that bag into the can," said Frank.

"Help!" yelled Judy.

"They can't hear us," said Andrew.

"HELP!" Judy screamed louder.

But no one heard her tiny voice as their bag hit the bottom of the garbage can.

FOUND . . . AND LOST

Smush!

Andrew's brain kerchunked against his skull when they landed.

Klunketa . . . klunketa . . . klunketa . . .

Andrew poked his head through the opening at the top of the bag. He watched as Frank and Jeff dragged the can out of the classroom, down the hall, and out of the school.

"What do we do now?" asked Judy.

"We'll find a way to get out of the bag and get back to the Goa Constrictor," said Andrew. "But first I've got to find the remote."

Andrew dug down through a rotten lettuce leaf. *Feels like Jell-O,* he thought. He shoved away some green peas and crawled through a bite mark in a pizza crust.

I wonder who chewed this, thought Andrew.

meep . . . "Gotta call Uncle Al," said Thudd. "He find way to help."

Uncle Al was Andrew and Judy's uncle. He was also a super-smart scientist who invented Thudd.

"Good idea, Thudd," said Andrew. "But I think Uncle Al is still delivering all those prehistoric animals back to their own times and places."

Thudd pressed the big purple button in the middle of his chest. This sent a signal to Uncle Al's Hologram Helper. The Hologram Helper allowed Uncle Al to get messages and to visit with people by hologram.

Thudd's purple button popped open and a beam of purple light flashed out.

A see-through, slightly purple picture of Uncle Al floated at the end of the beam.

"Hey there!" said the smiling see-through Uncle Al. "I'm away from my laboratory. Your message has reached my Hologram Helper. If you're calling to have a friendly chat, please press one. If you have discovered life on another planet, please press two. If you're calling to complain about the smells coming from my laboratory, please press three. If this is a purple-button emergency, please scream loudly. I will contact you as soon as possible."

"Yaaaaargh!" screamed Andrew. "We need help, Uncle Al!"

Andrew dug his way through sticky spaghetti and climbed over a carrot.

Andrew was crawling over an apple core when something caught his eye.

"I found the remote!" he shouted.

He reached for a dark object half hidden under a strand of spaghetti.

"Then let's get out of here," yelled Judy.

As Andrew reached for the dark thing, he saw what it really was.

"Um, we can't leave yet," he said. "All I found was Germy's Excuse-O-Matic."

Andrew put the gadget in his pants pocket.

Suddenly their garbage bag was yanked up.

"Toss 'er in!" said Frank.

The bag flew through the air and flopped onto a heap of bags in the rear of the truck.

"Yeeouch!" hollered Andrew. He tumbled over the sharp edge of an eggshell, fell into a blob of chocolate pudding, and got something hard stuck in his ear.

Judy smacked into a bread crust, got a Cheerio stuck in her hair, and plopped next to Andrew in the pudding blob.

When Andrew reached to pull the hard thing out of his ear, its shape felt familiar.

"The remote!" shouted Andrew. "I found it!"

"So how are we going to get back to school and get ourselves unshrunk now, Bug-Brain?" asked Judy.

Andrew looked around. He went over to the eggshell and broke off a piece.

"This shell has a sharp edge," he said. "We can use it to cut a hole in the bag and get out."

The doors of the garbage truck slammed.

meep . . . "Garbage truck can carry as much weight as six big elephants."

"Don't waste your batteries on elephants, Thudd," said Judy crossly. "Figure out how to get us unshrunk and unstinky."

meep . . . "Garbage stinky cuz little bacteria eat it," said Thudd. "Poop out stuff that make food for plants. Burp up stinky gas. If bacteria and fungus not eat garbage, earth be piled high, high, high with garbage and dead stuff."

Judy rolled her eyes.

"Okay, Frank," said Jeff, his voice drifting through the open windows of the truck's cab. "On to the dump."

A VERY UN-"HAPPY MEAL"

As the truck rumbled along the road, Andrew tried to saw through the plastic bag with a sliver of eggshell.

"If we can get out of the bag," he said, "we can find a place to stay on the truck till it goes back to school."

Andrew lurched as the garbage truck turned onto a narrow road. Through the clear plastic bag he could see a sign. It said CITY DUMP. An arrow pointed straight ahead.

Soon the truck pulled up alongside a strange building. Its walls were made of tires stacked on top of each other. A sign in front read:

STOP HERE BEFORE PROCEEDING TO THE DUMP.
THANK YOU!
HUGO WILSON, MANAGER

The yard in front of the tire building was covered with furniture and toys—rocking chairs, rocking horses, tables, mirror frames, and swings. And they were all made from tires!

"What a weird place!" said Judy.

meep . . . "Hugo Wilson famous," said Thudd. "Come up with lotsa ways to use old stuff."

"Mr. Wilson is friends with Uncle Al," said Andrew. "Uncle Al told me they've been figuring out how many ways they could recycle old tires.

"They chop up tires and use them to cover playgrounds with soft stuff so kids don't get hurt. They make floor tiles out of tires. They shred tires and mix them with cement to pave

roads so that they aren't slippery in the rain and snow. Mr. Wilson is a neat guy."

Near the door of the tire building were piles and piles of tires. There were regular-sized tires from cars, big tires from trucks and buses, and huge tires from tractors.

A tall man wearing a leather apron was cutting up a tire with an electric saw. A one-legged seagull was perched on his shoulder.

"G'day, mates!" the man called out. He turned off his saw.

"Hey, Hugo," said Jeff. "Want you to meet my new partner, Frank."

Hugo stretched out a big, strong hand to Frank.

"What are you up to here, Hugo?" asked Frank, waving his hand at the yard.

"Comin' up with ways to use old tires, mate," said Hugo. "Every year, we toss out a billion tires. If we lined 'em up, they'd circle the earth four times. They'd reach halfway to the moon. Can't have that!"

Hugo checked his watch. "It's feedin' time at the zoo. Have you got somethin' for my guys?"

"Something real juicy," said Jeff.

Judy peered through the garbage bag. "He's coming this way," she said. "Hurry up with that cutting!"

But it was too late. Andrew and Judy were tossed like a garbage salad as Jeff yanked their bag off the top of the pile.

"Yuck! Yuck! Yuck!" Judy griped as the bag bounced with Jeff's hurried steps. Jeff caught up with Hugo on the shady side of the tire building and handed him the bag.

"Thanks, mate," said Hugo. "First, I'd better feed Matilda so she won't be feasting on the zoo."

Hugo reached into his pocket and pulled out a peanut.

"Heads up, Matilda!" he said.

He tossed the peanut high into the air. The seagull caught it in her beak.

"Funny thing," said Hugo. "She doesn't eat the peanuts straightaway. Keeps 'em in her beak and flies off to the dump across the road. Bet she's got a nest there."

Jeff glanced at his watch. "Don't have time to visit the zoo today, Hugo," said Jeff. "We'd better unload and take off."

Hugo nodded. "Yours is a special load, fellas," he said. "It's the very last one for this place."

Jeff and Frank walked off toward the truck.

Lined up against the tire building were large plastic bins with lids. The lids were marked GIANT GIPPSLAND, TIGERS, OREGON GIANT, and RED WRIGGLERS.

Hugo laid the garbage bag on top of a bin and lifted the lid labeled RED WRIGGLERS. Andrew saw that the open bin was filled almost to the top with dirt, shredded newspapers, and leaves.

Hugo reached into the bin and pulled up a handful of squirming worms.

"You're lookin' good!" he said. "It's chow time!"

"Chow time!" said Judy. "The chow must be *us!*"

meep . . . "Oody and Drewd still too big for red wriggler worms to eat," said Thudd. "Hugo use worms to turn stinky garbage into super plant food. Worms eat garbage and paper. In one day, worm eat as much as worm weigh! Worm poop out stuff called 'castings.' Super food for plants."

Hugo scooped a hole in the dirt mixture and laid the worms gently into the bin.

The garbage bag jiggled. The tips of Hugo's big fingers were heading for Andrew!

"Yikes!" yelled Andrew.

He hid under the eggshell. A slice of gooey brown banana slid over him.

Kraaaack!

Andrew's eggshell snapped between Hugo's fingers! Hugo was dragging him up

with a handful of gross, disgusting garbage!

Hugo examined what he had pulled up. "Ah, yes," he said. "A 'Happy Meal' for worms—eggshells for calcium, greens for vitamins, bananas for dessert."

Andrew clawed frantically at the slimy banana slice. *If I can get out from under this yucky banana,* thought Andrew, *Hugo will see me and not throw us to the worms.*

Suddenly Andrew was falling again.

Splaaaaat!

EAT DIRT!

As Hugo dropped a handful of garbage into the bin, Andrew tumbled out of the eggshell and got smacked in the head by a green pea and slammed by a pickle.

"Ooofers!" yelled Andrew as he landed on a shred of newspaper. A damp-cellar smell filled his nose—the smell of dirt.

A shadow fell over the bin.

Hugo's big hands were heading down. They began to stir the garbage—and Andrew—into the dirt.

Andrew flicked on his flashlight. What could protect him from getting crushed by those giant fingers?

There's a peanut shell! thought Andrew. He scrambled under the igloo shape and scraped the dirt away. The fingers were pushing his peanut shell down and down!

Then the shell stopped moving. But other things were moving. It felt like rough hairbrushes were scratching Andrew's arms and legs.

Reddish brown worms that looked like bulgy garden hoses were tunneling through the garbage and dirt—and over Andrew!

"Yowzers!" yelled Andrew. "These guys are *scratchy*!"

meep . . . "Worms got bristles," said Thudd. "Use bristles to dig through dirt. Help worm to stick in wormhole, not get pulled out by bird."

One of the worms stopped in front of Andrew.

All Andrew could see was a brown flap.

meep . . . "Head of worm," said Thudd. "Worm not got eyes. Not got nose. Not got ears. But flap in front of mouth tell worm about light. Tell worm about smells. Worm feel stuff move."

The worm lifted its flap. Beneath was a mouth that looked like an inner tube. Dirt and bits of paper and lettuce were getting dragged into the mouth. It was like a vacuum cleaner!

meep . . . "Worm suck in dirt," said Thudd. "Eat bits of food and lotsa bacteria. Poop out castings."

Another worm wriggled up to Andrew's face and lifted its flap. Andrew tried to squirm out of the way, but the worm pressed its slimy, rubbery mouth against Andrew's nose.

"Yuck!" shouted Andrew. He tried to shove the worm's goocy flap away. "This worm is awfully strong!"

meep . . . "Worm is all muscle," said Thudd. "Worm lot stronger than same-sized human."

Thwap . . . *thwap* . . . *thwap* . . .

Something was pounding on the other side of the peanut shell.

"I *hear* you!" said a voice Andrew knew well.

"Judy!" said Andrew. "I need a little help here."

Judy crept around to the inside of the shell.

"*Eeeuw!*" she said when she saw the worm

sucking Andrew's nose. "It *loves* you!"

"Matilda, *NO!*" Andrew heard Hugo yell.

Suddenly something latched on to the peanut shell and shook it. The worm came loose from Andrew's nose. Andrew and Judy pulled the shell over themselves.

A fishy stink mixed with the smell of garbage and dirt. The peanut shell was going up like a fast elevator. The beam of Andrew's flashlight showed they were in a small space with curving yellow walls.

"Matilda!" shouted Hugo. "Hope you're not eatin' my hardworkin' worms! That's why I feed ya peanuts!"

But the seagull paid no attention to Hugo's shouts. It was flying off—with Andrew and Judy in its beak!

TWO WAYS TO GET DOWN IN THE DUMPS

"We'll be bird poop!" said Judy.

"Matilda hasn't swallowed us yet," said Andrew. "Maybe she'll figure out we're not a peanut."

meep . . . "Seagull got red spot on side of beak," said Thudd.

"Cheese Louise!" said Judy. "This is no time for seagull trivia, Thudd!"

meep . . . "Spot on beak help us get out, maybe," said Thudd. "When baby seagull want to eat, it peck at red spot on beak of big seagull. Make big seagull throw up food for baby bird to eat. If Drewd and Oody pound on inside of beak, maybe make seagull throw *us* up!"

"Super idea, Thudd!" said Andrew.

"Eeeeeuw!" said Judy. "Just thinking about it makes *me* want to throw up!"

Andrew put his arm around Judy. "It's either that or end up as bird poop on the windshield of someone's car," he said.

Andrew and Judy leaned as the seagull turned. It was flying slower. Their peanut shell smacked the front of the beak as the seagull landed at the dump.

meep . . . "Pound on side of beak!" squeaked Thudd. "Use shell!"

Andrew stepped onto the seagull's hard tongue.

"Grab the shell, Judy," said Andrew. "One . . . two . . . three!"

They slammed the peanut shell into the beak again and again.

There was rumbling down below. The beak cracked open.

Suddenly a wave of warm, lumpy, fishy soup tossed them out of the beak.

The seagull hopped into the air, spread its wings, and flew off.

"Oofers!" hollered Andrew. He landed on a jelly doughnut with bite marks.

"Aaaack!" yelled Judy. She tumbled onto the petal of a plastic daisy.

Judy sat up and spit stuff out of her mouth. *"Ploof! Ploof! PLOOOF!"*

She wiped her face with her sleeve. But since she was entirely soaked with seagull vomit, it didn't help.

"What did you say?" asked Andrew.

"Can't hear what you're saying!" shouted Judy, pulling bits of fish out of her hair. "It's so *loud* here!"

The air was stuffed with sound. A spiral of screaming seagulls filled the afternoon sky. Crickets were making such a racket, Andrew felt he had crickets in his ears. Flies whizzed and whined like small airplanes above their heads.

A fly circled Andrew's doughnut and came in for a landing. The fly's dark eyes covered most of its head like two big helmets. Each eye looked like it was made up of thousands of tiny tiles. The fly crept over the doughnut in slow circles.

meep . . . "Fly taste stuff with feet," said Thudd.

A shadow passed over the doughnut. A black crow, looking as big as a jet plane, swooped low. The fly zoomed off.

An explosion of umbrella shapes shot off the ground, whizzed high into the air, and rained back down.

meep . . . "Springtail bug!" said Thudd. "Got springs under back legs. Jump high, high, high! Like human jumping over ten-story building!"

"Holy moly!" yelled Andrew as a fuzzy-headed gray springtail landed on his shoulder. It looked like a big parrot. The prickly antennas

between its bumpy black eyes tickled Andrew's ear. Through his shirt, Andrew felt the springtail's feet clawing his back.

As Andrew struggled to shove the bug off, another one landed in his lap.

"Yaaaaah!" screamed Judy, fighting off the springtails that had rained down on her.

Trying to get away, she fell off her petal and onto the ground.

"YAAAAAAAAH!" she screamed at the top of her lungs. "It's *horrible* down here!"

9 BEETLE-MANIA!

Andrew fought off the springtails and crept to the edge of the doughnut.

"Jeepers creepers!" he whispered as he checked out the scene on the ground.

Shiny beetles twice as big as Andrew were hurrying about on thorny legs like bizarre armored vehicles. Some of them were burrowing into underground tunnels.

A giant-headed black ant was hauling a dead bug on its back. A dozen tiny red ants had circled a green Froot Loop and were carrying it away.

"It's like the dismissal bell rang in bug world!" said Andrew.

Beneath the beetles, the ground was a squirming carpet of wormy things big and small. Beside Andrew's doughnut, a heap of little white worms wriggled over a fish head.

meep . . . "Baby blowflies," said Thudd. "Mother blowfly lay eggs on dead meat. Egg hatch into maggot. Maggot look like worm. Maggot never eat living stuff. Only eat dead meat."

"*HELP!*" Judy was screaming.

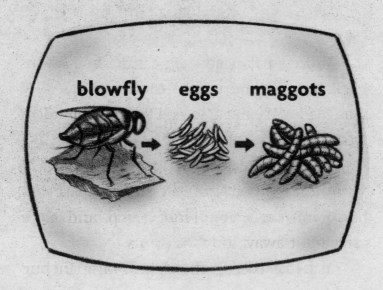

blowfly   eggs   maggots

"I'm coming!" yelled Andrew.

As he was about to climb down the doughnut, he turned back and grabbed the peanut shell.

"We might need this," he said, tossing it onto the ground. It landed on the maggots.

When Andrew reached the ground, he dragged the peanut shell away from the maggots. Some of them stuck to the shell. He pushed them off.

"These guys feel like a squishy toy," he said.

Andrew balanced the peanut shell on his back the way he would carry a canoe. He chuckled. "I'll bet I look like some kind of weird beetle."

meep . . . "Peanut beetle," said Thudd.

Andrew tried not to step on worms, bump into bugs, or fall into beetle holes as he clomped toward Judy's screams.

As he hiked past the mouth of a ketchup

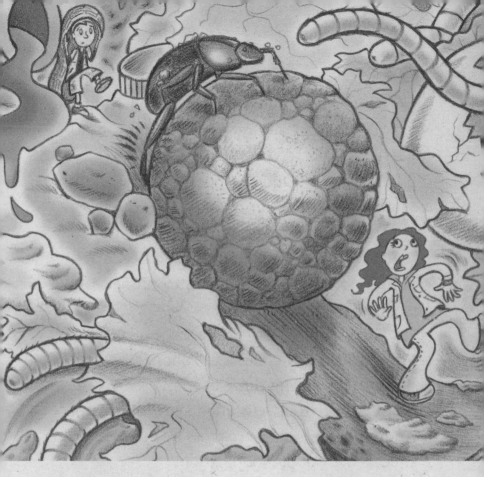

bottle, he spotted Judy. She was skidding and sliding over a slice of moldy meat.

A rough brown ball, two times as high as Judy, was rolling behind her. A beetle was behind the ball, pushing it. The strange beetle ball was about to run Judy over!

meep . . . "Dung beetle!" squeaked Thudd.

"Huh?" said Andrew, scrambling toward Judy.

meep . . . "Dung is poop," said Thudd. "Dung beetles live on poop.

"Male dung beetle find poop. Give it to female dung beetle. Female dung beetle roll poop into big ball. Roll ball into tunnel. Lay egg in poop ball.

"Egg hatch into little wormy thing. Worm called larva. Larva eat poop. Grow up. Become big, strong dung beetle."

A silver trail glistened just ahead of Andrew. He was about to cross it when Thudd squeaked, "Noop! Noop! Noop!"

"What's the matter, Thudd?" asked Andrew.

meep . . . "Shiny stuff is slime," said Thudd. "Slime from giant banana slug. Sticky, sticky, sticky! Like glue! Drewd step, Drewd stuck."

"Hmmm . . . ," said Andrew. He looked

around, found a leaf, laid it across the slime
trail, and hurried toward Judy.

Just as Andrew got to Judy, she slipped on
the slimy slice of meat. The poop ball was
touching her toes!

In a split second, Andrew grabbed his
peanut shell and used it to give Judy a big
shove.

Andrew held his breath.

The globe of poop rolled past. An un-
squashed Judy was lying next to a plastic
spoon.

"Super-duper pooper-scooper!" cheered
Andrew.

"That stupid dung beetle almost ran me
over with its stupid poop ball!" said Judy,
sitting up on the edge of the spoon.

"You know about dung beetles?" said
Andrew.

"Of course," said Judy. "Grandpa gave me
tons of great stuff from his beetle collection.
I know *everything* about beetles."

Judy tried to scrape meat slime off her jacket. "Yeuw!" she said. "Now I smell even worse."

meep . . . "Good thing about bad smell," said Thudd. "In little while, nose not smell bad smell so much. Nose stop sending signal to brain."

"Stuff a stinky sock in it, Thudd," said Judy, scanning the ground.

She snatched a bread crumb away from three small red ants and wiped meat goo off her face.

Amid the noise of birds and bugs, Andrew thought he heard a rustling sound. He turned to see something long and narrow speeding toward them. It was going so fast it was almost a blur!

THE CANNIBALS ARE COMING!

"Eeek!" squeaked Thudd. "Centipede! Centipede is meat-eater. Drewd and Oody gotta hide! Flip spoon!"

Judy leapt off the spoon. She and Andrew flipped it over and hid under the bowl. They peered out from under the edge. The centipede's long antennas were wagging. Fang-like claws under its mouth opened like scissors. Its spiky legs moved as smoothly as a wave.

"Look!" said Andrew. "There's another one chasing it!"

meep . . . "Centipede is cannibal," said Thudd. "Try to eat other centipede."

Suddenly legs started falling off the first

centipede. And those legs kept moving all by themselves!

"Wowzers schnauzers!" said Andrew. "Legs on the loose!"

meep . . . "When centipede chased by predator, centipede toss legs," said Thudd. "Try to confuse predator. Can grow legs back."

The second centipede came so close to the spoon that Andrew saw the sharp claws at the tips of its legs. The centipede's last long

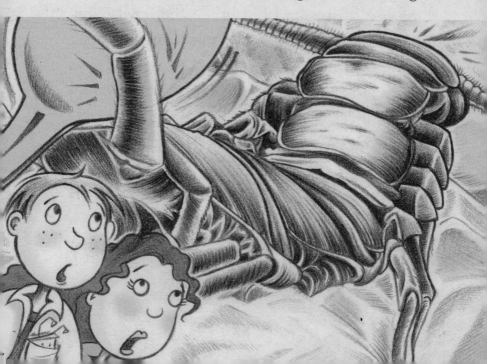

legs whipped by—and knocked the spoon off Andrew and Judy. Both centipedes disappeared behind a watermelon rind.

"Wowzers schnauzers!" sighed Andrew. "I'm glad *that's* over!"

"Okay, Bug-Brain," said Judy. "The sun is going down. We've got to get out of this dump before dark. That's when really awful things come out—skunks, foxes, even *bats!* *Eeeeuw!*" Judy shivered.

"We have to find a high place," said Andrew, looking around. "If we can see Hugo's building, then we can figure out how to get there."

The craggy ground around them was buzzing with flies. There was a teacup, watermelon rinds, a broken eggbeater, and a birthday card smeared with mustard.

"I can climb the—" Andrew began, when suddenly he felt the ground below him coming up!

TIME TO CRY WOLF!

A round trapdoor beneath Andrew and Judy was pushing up! From under the door crept five long, hairy legs.

"Uh-oh," groaned Andrew.

"Eeeeeeyaaaaaaah!" hollered Judy, hands clapped over her mouth.

"Eeek! Wolf spider!" squeaked Thudd.

"Let's get out of here before we see the rest of it," said Andrew.

"With legs like that," said Judy in a shaky voice, "it can run a lot faster than we can."

meep . . . "Got giant poison fangs!" squeaked Thudd. "Drewd and Oody gotta run across slug-slime trail. Remember, trail sticky, sticky, sticky! No touch! Use leaf to cross. When spider walk on slime trail, feet get stuck."

Andrew grabbed Judy's arm. "Let's go!" he said.

Andrew and Judy picked and tripped their way through wormy strawberries, soft black potatoes, and moldy cheese chunks.

Andrew heard soft shuffling behind them and turned to see.

Not more than five inches behind them was a giant hairy head with two black eyes on top, two big eyes below them, and a row of four small eyes below those.

Most horrible of all were the two huge, fuzzy orange fangs that hung almost to the ground.

Andrew could barely breathe.

Blocking the way ahead of them was a black and orange beetle.

"Cheese Louise!" said Judy. "That's a bombardier beetle!"

Judy turned to see where the spider was. Two inches away!

"We'll never make it to the slime trail," she gasped. "Time for plan B. Step away from the butt of the beetle."

Judy snatched up a cherry stem, whacked the beetle's behind, and dove under a leaf.

The beetle swiveled its rear end.

Popetta! Popetta! Popetta!

With loud pops, a cloud of blue smoke exploded from the beetle's behind. A steaming spray that stunk worse than burning rubber shot into the air.

"Ack!" gagged Andrew.

"Gack! Gack! Gack!" coughed Judy.

meep . . . "Bombardier beetle make boiling-hot stinky stuff!" said Thudd. "Shoot stinky stuff one thousand times every second!"

Through burning, watery eyes, Andrew saw the spider stop. It reared up on its back legs! It looked like it was about to attack! But

instead, it backed away, swiveled around, raced into its tunnel, and pulled its trapdoor shut.

The bombardier beetle spread its wings and took off.

"Whew!" said Judy, rubbing her eyes. "I'm sure glad Grandpa taught me about beetles."

"Don't rub your eyes," said Andrew. "They'll just hurt more."

Judy kept on rubbing. "So let's get back to getting out of the dump," she said.

Andrew pointed ahead.

"That eggbeater there is the highest thing near us," he said. "I'll climb it. Maybe I can tell where we are."

Andrew crept up to one of the beaters and tried to climb up. But it was too smooth and slippery.

"Hmmmm . . . ," he mumbled.

Andrew walked back to the slug's slime

trail and scooped some slime up with his hands.

"Wowzers!" he said. "This stuff is really sticky! It feels like rubber cement."

Andrew went back to the eggbeater and began climbing. His sticky hands made it easy. He quickly reached the top.

"See anything?" Judy yelled up.

"Nothing yet," said Andrew, looking around. "Hey! I see a sign!"

"Sign shmine," said Judy. "Someone threw out a sign. So what?"

"This sign says GARBOLOGISTS AT WORK!" said Andrew excitedly.

meep . . . "*Garbologist* mean 'someone who study garbage,'" said Thudd.

"The sign is next to a big hole in the ground," said Andrew.

"Do you see people?" asked Judy.

"Nope," said Andrew. "Maybe they're in the hole studying garbage. Let's go see!"

Andrew climbed down the eggbeater and led the way, trying to step on as few worms as possible.

In a few minutes, they arrived at the sign.

Andrew crept toward the edge of the hole.

"YES!" he said. *"*There's two heads down there!*"*

A BIG BAT-TLE

"Looks like a blond guy and a girl with long brown hair," said Judy, peering into the hole. "They can get us out of here!"

Andrew got down on all fours and leaned over the edge. Judy knelt next to him. "Looks like the guy is putting something into a plastic bag," she said. "I can hear them talking."

"This is exciting!" the guy said.

"What is it, Cody?" asked the girl.

"A newspaper from July 20, 1969," said Cody. "Neil Armstrong Walks on the Moon."

"My gosh!" said the girl. "Imagine reading a newspaper from so long ago."

meep . . . "When paper get buried," said Thudd, "take long time to get eaten by worms and stuff. Long time to turn into good dirt.

"Plastic worse. Plastic last forever. Nothing eat plastic to make dirt."

Down in the hole, Cody was asking Hannah a question. "What's the most interesting thing that you found, Hannah?" he said.

Hannah held up a strange-looking container. "This whale-oil lamp," she said. "It's from about 1880. Imagine eating dinner or reading books by the light of burning whale fat."

Cody nodded. "Garbage dumps are history books," he said. "You can tell a lot about the way people lived from the stuff they threw away."

"This place has been used as a dump for hundreds of years," said Hannah. "If we had more time to dig, I'll bet we'd find arrowheads and stone tools."

"We'll never know," said Cody. "They'll begin to bulldoze the dump tomorrow. Then they'll cover it with clean dirt and grass."

Hannah shook her head. "It's hard to believe they're turning the dump into a park!"

"Cheese Louise!" said Judy. "We're going to get *bulldozed and buried!*"

"The new landfill will be cleaner than this dump," Hannah was saying. "But it's going to use up a tremendous amount of land. And they're building it close to the school, too."

The sun was quickly sinking into a bright pink and orange glow.

Cody looked up. "It'll be dark soon," he said. "Let's pack our backpacks and get out of here."

Andrew looked Judy in the eye. "This is dangerous," he said. "But we don't have a choice. As Cody and Hannah come up the ladder, we jump onto one of their backpacks."

"What if we miss when we jump?" Judy

asked. "We'll be lost in that hole and never get out."

The racket of the day was changing into the noises of the night—quieter noises, spookier noises.

"My hands are still super-sticky from the slug slime," said Andrew. "I'll stick to whatever I touch. Wrap your arms around my waist. We'll jump together and I'll grab on to Cody or Hannah when they come up."

It was getting dark. Colors were fading to black and white. Most of the seagulls were gone. But a flurry of small, dark shapes were darting and diving in the sky.

meep . . . "Bats!"

"*Eeeuw!*" Judy shuddered. "We'll never make it through the night here."

"Okay," said Andrew. "Jump when I say 'Go.'"

Cody climbed so quickly that he was out of the hole before they were ready.

"Oh no!" said Judy.

"We have one more chance," said Andrew.

Hannah was climbing up.

Judy leaned over to get a better look.

Andrew lost his balance, and they toppled into the hole!

"Errrgh!" hollered Andrew as they tumbled down and down.

"Aaaaaack!" screamed Judy.

Booof!

Andrew felt himself sinking into something as soft as a feather pillow but stringy.

"We've landed in Hannah's hair!" he said.

Hannah stopped climbing. Her brown hair ruffled and separated into strands. Fingertips were rushing toward them!

"Super-duper pooper-scooper!" yelled Andrew. "She *feels* us! She'll find us! We're saved! I can even get back in time to win the Young Inventors Contest!"

Hannah's slender fingers combed through her long, soft hair.

"Oook! Bugs!" she said as Andrew got poked in the stomach by her pink fingernail.

Andrew and Judy were caught between her fingers! They were getting swept away!

"Help us, Hannah!" they screamed, but she couldn't hear them.

She flicked her fingers, flinging Andrew and Judy into the air.

"Aaaaargh!" yelled Andrew.

"Aaaaaaaaah!" yelled Judy.

"Eeek!" squeaked Thudd.

Everything was a blur to Andrew as he tumbled through the air. But he caught sight of a shadow diving toward him. The shadow had giant pointy ears and needle teeth.

A bat! thought Andrew. *To a bat, we're bugs! Bats can eat their weight in bugs every night!*

Desperate to get away, Andrew flapped his arms and legs as though he were swimming.

"Arghhhhhhhhh!" Andrew yelled as he whammed into something hard and furry. He grabbed on to the fur.

When he saw the huge pointy ear blocking his view, Andrew knew he had landed on the back of a bat!

The way the bat dove and spun, zigged and zagged, was crazier than any rollercoaster ride.

"Eeeeeeeeeee!"

The eerie cry came from the other side of
the bat.

It was Judy! She was hanging off the bat's
other ear!

"Judy!" yelled Andrew. "At least we're
leaving the dump before dark!"

TO BE CONTINUED IN ANDREW, JUDY, AND THUDD'S
NEXT EXCITING ADVENTURE:

ANDREW LOST
WITH THE BATS!

In stores July 2006

THUDD

TRUE STUFF

Thudd wanted to tell you more about garbage, but he was awfully busy trying to keep Andrew and Judy from being eaten by centipedes and wolf spiders. Here's what he wanted to say:

• A person who designs buildings is called an architect. An architect named Michael Reynolds designs buildings with outside walls made out of recycled tires filled with dirt. These thick walls keep the building warm in winter and cool in summer.

• If you stay in a stinky place, in a few minutes you won't even notice the smell. The smell hasn't gone away. Your brain just stops paying attention to the signals from your nose.

• Like us, worms need oxygen. But worms don't breathe the way we do. Instead, oxygen from the air dissolves in the wet slime on their bodies. Then the oxygen passes through the worm's skin into its body.

We have something in common with worms. Our lungs must always be wet. When we breathe air into our lungs, the oxygen dissolves in the wetness and passes into our blood.

• If a worm loses its rear end, the head end can grow another rear end. But a worm's rear end can't grow another head.

• Using worms to turn paper and garbage into super-nutritious food for plants is called vermicomposting. The *vermi* part of the word means "worm." Vermicomposting is easy and fun. You might want to try it. In "Where to

Find More True Stuff," you'll find a book that tells you how to do it.

• Maggots—baby flies that look like small worms—are used to cure dangerous infections. When doctors put maggots on the wound, these wormy little guys munch on the infected skin and any other dead tissue. They clean the wound completely and leave the healthy tissue alone. And the maggots' saliva kills deadly bacteria! Imagine— someday your life could be saved by maggots!

• Because young dung beetles hatch from what looks like a ball of lifeless dirt, ancient Egyptians thought dung beetles had the power to create life and even to bring life to the dead.

One of the most powerful Egyptian gods was called Ra. He rolled the sun across the sky every day, and he could bring the dead back to life. Ancient Egyptian artists sometimes drew pictures of Ra in the shape of a dung beetle.

• Garbage gets slimy, smells stinky, and turns weird colors. These changes are caused by bacteria, funguses, and molds. These guys break garbage down and turn it back into molecules that living things can use for food. Without bacteria, funguses, and molds, the earth would be piled hundreds of miles high with garbage and dead things.

• The word *centipede* means "hundred feet." (*Centi* means "hundred" and *pede* means "feet.") But whoever named centipedes must not have been counting carefully. Different kinds of centipedes have from thirty to over 300 feet!

• *Millipede* means "thousand feet." (*Milli* means "thousand.") But the millipede with the most feet has *only* 750!

THUDD

WHERE TO FIND MORE TRUE STUFF

Would you like to become a garbologist? Or maybe you just like to read about trashy stuff. If so, here are some books you might enjoy:

• *Life in a Garbage Dump* by Jill Bailey (Chicago: Raintree, 2004). You'll find out about everything that lives in dumps—from bacteria and funguses to snakes and bears. Lots of interesting facts and things to do.

• *Garbage! Where It Comes From, Where It Goes* by Evan and Janet Hadingham (New York: Simon and Schuster, 1990). Lots of information about what people around the world do with their garbage. Watch out! This can get pretty strange.

- *Pee Wee's Great Adventure: A Guide to Vermi-composting* by Larraine Roulston (Kalamazoo, MI: Flowerfield Enterprises/Flower Press, 2004). This short booklet tells an amusing story about a worm's life with other creatures in a compost heap. It also gives instructions for vermicomposting, using worms to recycle garbage and paper into great plant food. To find this booklet, go to www.wormdigest.org or other vermicomposting Web sites.

- *There's a Hair in My Dirt: A Worm's Story* by Gary Larson (New York: HarperCollins, 1998). What would worms think about the world if they could think? Very funny and very wise!

Turn the page
for a sneak peek at
Andrew, Judy, and Thudd's
next exciting adventure—

ANDREW LOST
WITH THE BATS!

Available July 2006

1 GOING BATTY

"Yaaaaargh!" hollered tiny Andrew Dubble. He was as big as a beetle and hanging on to the back of a bat.

The bat zigged and zagged and zoomed through the twilight sky. It was searching for its dinner of bugs.

The wind stung Andrew's eyes, tugged his scalp, and blew him backward. Every zig and zag made Andrew's stomach slosh. *Urf!* he thought. *I feel like throwing up.*

URRRRRP!

Andrew popped out a big, garlicky burp. *It's the pepperoni pizza from lunch,* he thought.

He gripped the soft fur of the bat's neck tighter.

meep . . . "Drewd okey-dokey?" came a squeaky voice from Andrew's shirt pocket. "Drewd hit by mosquito stinger."

It was Thudd, Andrew's little silver robot and best friend.

"I'm as okay as anyone hanging off a bat can be," said Andrew. "But it's like the worst roller-coaster ride ever and there's no safety belt!"

"Androooooooo!" came a wail from the other side of the bat.

It was Judy Dubble, Andrew's thirteen-year-old cousin. She was dangling from the tip of one of the bat's big ears like an earring.

"Jooodeeeeee!" hollered Andrew, trying to make his little voice heard over the wind. "Get onto the back of the bat! You won't flap around so much!"

"Whaaaat?" yelled Judy. "I can hardly

hear you! I'm trying to get off this stupid ear!"

Judy reached for the bat's neck with one hand and grabbed a fistful of fur. Her eyes squeezed into slits as her other hand let go of the ear.

Suddenly Judy was bouncing like a rodeo cowgirl off the neck of the bat. One hand waved frantically in the air.

Finally, Judy grabbed a clump of bat fur with her free hand. She climbed up the bat's neck and tucked herself in behind one of the bat's ears.

The air swarmed with specks and dots flying like dizzy airplanes. Sometimes Andrew could make out what they were—mosquitoes, beetles, moths.

Nyeeeeeee . . .

A high-pitched whine hurt Andrew's ears.

meep . . . "Mosquito!" said Thudd.

Bring magic into your life with these enchanting books!

Magic Tree House® series
by Mary Pope Osborne

The Magic Elements Quartet
by Mallory Loehr
Water Wishes
Earth Magic
Wind Spell
Fire Dreams

Dragons
by Lucille Recht Penner

Fox Eyes
by Mordicai Gerstein

King Arthur's Courage
by Stephanie Spinner

The Magic of Merlin
by Stephanie Spinner

Unicorns
by Lucille Recht Penner